The Small Dragon

With thanks to Alex and Edward

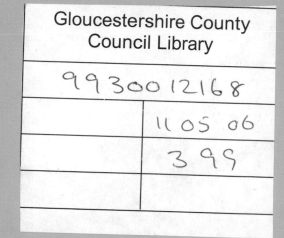
First published 2005
Evans Brothers Limited
2A Portman Mansions
Chiltern Street
London W1U 6NR

British Library Cataloguing in Publication Data
Swallow, Su
        Sand Dragon. – (Twisters)
        1. Children's stories – Pictorial works
        I. Title
        823.9'14 [J]

13-digit ISBN (from 1 January 2007) 9780237529420

Printed in China by WKT Company Limited

Series Editor: Nick Turpin
Design: Robert Walster
Production: Jenny Mulvanny
Series Consultant: Gill Matthews

TWISTERS

The Sand
Dragon

Su Swallow
and Silvia Raga

Evans

The seaside!

5

Splish splash!

Look!

Hurray!

"What's that?" said Mum.

13

"A sand dragon."
They both went home.

15

16

The waves splashed,

the dragon swam,

19

and nibbled,

and danced.

23

The waves moved back.

24

The dragon lay on the
sand to dry.

Edward came back.

29

"Mummy, my sand dragon
hasn't moved all night!"

31

Why not try reading another Twisters book?